Bailey, the Wonder Dog

Look for all
the books in the

PET RESCUE CLUB
series

1 A New Home for Truman

2 No Time for Hallie

3 The Lonely Pony

4 Too Big to Run

5 A Puppy Called Disaster

6 Champion's New Shoes

7 A Purr-fect Pair

ASPCA kids
PET RESCUE CLUB

Bailey, the Wonder Dog

by Brenda Scott Royce
illustrated by Dana Regan

studio fun
INTERNATIONAL

Cover Illustration by Steve James

Studio Fun International
An imprint of Printers Row Publishing Group
A division of Readerlink Distribution Services, LLC
10350 Barnes Canyon Road, Suite 100, San Diego, CA 92121
www.studiofun.com

Library of Congress Cataloging-in-Publication Data is available on request.

ISBN 978-0-7944-4066-4
Manufactured, printed, and assembled in Shaoguan, China. SL/08/17.
21 20 19 18 17 1 2 3 4 5

***The American Society for the Prevention of Cruelty to Animals® (ASPCA®)
will receive 4% - 5% from the sale of ASPCA products, with a minimum
guarantee of $50,000, through December 2019.**

Comments? Questions? Call us at: 1-888-217-3346

To Xiana, Anthony, Cara, and Brandon

—B. S. R.

Career Day

"Zach's mom is up next!" Janey Whitfield cheered from her front-row seat at the school assembly.

Next to her, Lolli Simpson nodded with excitement. "She's got the coolest job of them all."

The gymnasium was decorated with large banners reading CAREER DAY. More than a dozen local professionals had turned up to participate in the event, each giving a ten-minute presentation about their job.

The kids had already heard from a newspaper reporter, an auto mechanic, and a librarian, when Dr. Goldman, the town's veterinarian, approached the podium. She wore her white lab coat over a lavender blouse and black pants.

"Good morning, students," she said into the microphone. "Before I begin my talk, I'm curious . . . how many of you have considered a career in veterinary medicine?"

Janey thrust her hand into the air. She wasn't exactly sure what she wanted to be when she grew up, but she hoped it would involve working with animals. She could imagine herself becoming a vet or a zookeeper or a horse trainer. Maybe even a marine biologist. There were lots of possibilities.

She wasn't surprised to see that Lolli had also raised her hand. Their love of animals was one of many things the two girls had in common. Along with their friends Zach Goldman and Adam Santos,

Janey and Lolli had formed the Pet Rescue Club to help the town's animals in need. They had reunited lost pets with their owners, found new homes for several animals, and recently helped a disabled dog walk on all fours for the very first time.

Janey swiveled around to look at Zach and Adam, who were seated together in the second row. Adam, who at age nine already had a successful dog-walking business, had his hand in the air, but Zach did not. "One vet in the family is enough," he said with a wink.

"The life of a veterinarian is seldom glamorous, but it can be very rewarding," Dr. Goldman was saying. She clicked a button on a remote, and a large photograph appeared on the screen behind her. Janey and Lolli giggled at the image of Dr. Goldman in mud-splattered overalls and work boots, standing next to the backside of a cow. "Most of my patients are small pets—dogs, cats, birds, rodents, and even some reptiles. But occasionally I get called out to local farms, as in the case of this cow who needed help delivering her calf."

As she clicked through a series of photographs of past patients, Dr. Goldman spoke about the training she went through to become a vet, and described some of the more unusual cases she had handled. A funny moment came when she put an X-ray on screen. "This was one of my first patients—a puppy who got into his owner's purse and swallowed a bunch of items, including some spare change. The owner hadn't even gotten around to naming him yet, but after his surgery she decided to call him Eighteen. Can anyone figure out why?"

"The surgery took eighteen hours?" a boy in the third row guessed, but Dr. Goldman shook her head.

Other students asked if the dog lived on Eighteenth Street or whether his surgery occurred on the eighteenth of the month. "Those are great guesses," Dr. Goldman responded, "but neither is correct."

Janey wrinkled her nose as she stared at the projected X-ray. The image showed a side view of the puppy, from its snout to its tail.

Among the foreign objects in its stomach, she could see the outlines of several coins. Judging by their size, it looked like a dime, a nickel, and three pennies. "I know, I know!" she said, raising her hand. She waited for Dr. Goldman to call her name before pointing to the X-ray and solving the mystery: "He swallowed eighteen cents."

. . . .

"I don't have any pets, but I feed the ducks in the pond behind my house every day," said Miss Evelyn Wakefield when she took the podium. "I'm here to talk about careers in music." As a church music director, Miss Evelyn selected the hymns for services, played piano, and oversaw the choir. She told the kids about her career path and encouraged those with an interest in music to follow their passion. Then she turned the mic over to Brian Mulligan, owner of Mulligan's Bakery.

"I didn't prepare a slide show," Mr. Mulligan said when he approached the podium. "But I did bring some samples."

The children cheered as bakery employees in pink T-shirts began passing out mini-cupcakes to everyone in the audience. Adam bit into his and grinned. "Raspberry swirl with dark chocolate chips. Magnificent!"

Zach was most intrigued by the last speaker, Police Chief Mario Pedroche, who regaled the children with thrilling stories of his career in law enforcement. The chief's gold badge glinted against his navy blue uniform.

When the assembly was over, the guests stayed to mingle with the students and answer their questions. Adam made a

beeline for the bakery owner, while Zach approached the police chief. "I think I'd make a good police detective," he told Chief Pedroche. "It seems like an awesome job."

The chief patted the boy's shoulder. "Do you have a knack for fact-finding and problem-solving? Are you willing to put in long hours chasing down leads?" Zach nodded enthusiastically, and the chief recommended books he could read and websites to visit for more information.

As he was chatting with the chief, Zach saw his mother approaching with her arms opened wide. He groaned and rolled his eyes. He'd die of embarrassment if she hugged him here, in front of all his friends. She surprised him by embracing the chief instead, standing on her tiptoes to hug the tall man.

"Good to see you, Chief," said Dr. Goldman. "It's been a long time."

The chief nodded. "It's been almost a year since Maggie died."

"She was a good girl. One of my best patients. I'll bet you miss her."

The chief's eyes welled with tears, but he managed to keep his voice steady. "Every day."

Janey and Lolli joined them. Both girls were holding pamphlets from the various career booths they'd visited.

"Where's Adam?" Zach asked them.

"I saw him talking to the baker, Mr. Mulligan," Lolli answered. "Probably trying to score an extra cupcake."

After introducing the girls to the chief, Dr. Goldman told the kids, "I treated the chief's German shepherd, Maggie, for many years. Do you remember her, Zach?"

"Isn't she the dog that was always hanging around the police station?"

"Yes." The chief smiled at the memory. "I used to bring her to work sometimes. The station staff loved having her around. The place hasn't been the same since. . . . "

"Maybe it's time for a new dog," Janey offered helpfully. "My friends and I volunteer at the Third Street Animal Shelter. There are lots of dogs there that need homes."

"It's true," Zach added. "I'm sure one of them would make a great police pooch."

"No, no. I don't think I'll ever adopt another animal." The chief tapped the left side of his chest, right under his badge. "No one could replace Maggie in my heart." He smiled at the children and then started to back away. "Good to see you, Doc. I have to get back to the station."

. . . .

Adam caught up with the others as they were filing out of the gymnasium. He told them that after talking to Mr. Mulligan, he was considering becoming a baker.

"I thought you wanted to be a vet," Janey said. "You love animals."

Adam turned both hands palm up and shrugged. "I also love cake."

"Hey, that gives me an idea," Lolli said. "You know how we're always trying to raise money for the shelter? Let's have a bake sale."

"Sweet!" Zach said, and Janey nodded in agreement. "Count me in."

"Me, too." Adam stroked his chin thoughtfully. "Maybe I'll create my own original cookie recipe."

2

Club Meeting

"Well, what do you think?" Adam's gaze ping-ponged between his friends' faces as they tried his first batch of homemade cookies. He'd created the recipe himself, using some of his favorite ingredients—peppermint, pistachios, and black licorice.

It was Saturday morning and they were holding a meeting of the Pet Rescue Club. The weather was picnic-perfect so they'd agreed to meet in the park. The four club members were sitting under the shade of a huge oak tree along with Lolli's dog, Roscoe. Part rottweiler, part Labrador, and part who-knows-what-else, the big mutt was one of the club's official mascots.

"I'm sorry, Adam," Janey said, frowning at her friend. "But they're not . . . very good."

"They're terrible!" Zach sputtered, gagged, and clutched at his throat. "Tastes like charcoal and chalk. *Blech!*"

Adam turned his attention to Lolli, who was still chewing. He could tell from her sour expression that she shared Zach's and Janey's opinion, but he knew she'd try not to hurt his feelings. When she swallowed, she simply said, "I don't think we should sell these at the bake sale."

"Sell them?" Zach teased. "We'd have to pay people to eat them."

Adam sighed. He knew the cookies weren't as good as the ones Mr. Mulligan sold in his bakery, but they didn't taste like charcoal and chalk. Did they?

Zach placed half of his cookie on the ground in front of Roscoe, but after sniffing it, the big mutt turned away, resting his head on his front paws. "Look, Roscoe doesn't want it—and dogs eat anything."

"Even spare change," Janey said, remembering the X-ray Zach's mother had shown them at the Career Day assembly. Since Dr. Goldman's talk, Janey was more certain than ever that she wanted to pursue a career working with animals.

"Roscoe's spoiled." Lolli patted her dog's head. "My parents and I bake him organic treats at home."

"You should make some of those for the bake sale," Janey suggested, and Lolli agreed. She also volunteered to make homemade muffins using her family's farm-grown blueberries.

Janey opened her notebook and turned to a blank page. She wrote BAKE SALE in block letters at the top and then started making a list of action items. "I'll bake some brownies," she said.

"Put me down for two-dozen cookies," Adam said. Before his friends could object, he added, "I promise to perfect my recipe in time for the bake sale. When is the bake sale, by the way?"

Janey shrugged. "We'll have to check with Kitty." Kitty was their favorite worker at the Third Street Animal Shelter. "I was thinking we could hold the sale on the sidewalk in front of the shelter, on a Saturday or Sunday, when lots of people are out shopping. Kitty can let us know which day would be best."

"If we need to wait for Adam to learn how to bake, that could take years," Zach said, rolling onto his side and laughing.

"Let's talk about publicity," Janey said, her pen poised in the air above her notebook. "How will we let people know about the sale?"

Lolli raised her hand. "Remember that reporter who spoke at Career Day? We could ask her to put something in the newspaper."

"Great idea," Janey said. "And I'll write about it on my blog." Janey had started her blog, Janey's Pet Place, as a way to get people to share cute animal pictures. Now, the Pet Rescue Club also used the blog to help animals in need.

A few minutes later, a station wagon pulled to a stop near the park. Roscoe's ears perked at the familiar honk of the car's horn.

Lolli looked over and saw her father waving from the driver's seat. "Time to go. Come on, Roscoe. Do any of you need a ride home?"

Adam stood and brushed leaves from his jeans. "No thanks. I have to go walk some dogs that live just up the street."

Zach hooked a thumb in Janey's direction. "We're going to walk to my mother's office. She said she'd drive us both home when she finishes with her patients." Zach and Janey were practically neighbors, living just a block apart. So it was often convenient for one of their parents to give both kids a ride.

They waved goodbye to Adam, Lolli, and Roscoe, and headed in the direction of Dr. Goldman's office. The sun was high in the sky, and birds were singing in the trees. At the corner of Bailey and Main Street, Zach looked both ways before entering the crosswalk.

"Hurry up, slow poke," he said, looking over his shoulder at Janey, who had stopped on the street corner, a funny expression on her face.

"Do you hear that?" she asked him, the frown lines on her face deepening.

Zach returned to Janey's side and listened. At first, he heard nothing but the sound of distant cars and the chatter of people entering and exiting the gym on the corner. Then, just when he was about to tell Janey to clean the wax from her ears, he heard something. A strange sound was coming from behind the building—a high-pitched whimper that was so faint he might have thought he'd imagined it, except Janey heard it, too. "Who—or what—is that?" he asked her.

"I don't know." She turned in the direction of the sound and gestured for Zach to follow. "But we have to find out."

3

Touch and Go

Zach and Janey followed the strange sound to the alley that ran behind the gym. "It's coming from over there," Zach said, pointing to a large dumpster to the left of the gym's rear entrance.

As they approached, the sound grew louder. Zach climbed on top of an overturned milk crate and peered down into the dumpster. There were a few bulging garbage bags as well as some loose trash, but nothing that could have made the weird noise. "Nothing but gross garbage in here," he said, wrinkling his nose at the smell.

Janey walked to the other side of the dumpster and let out a gasp. A battered cardboard box was wedged into the narrow space between the side of the dumpster and the brick building. A tattered green blanket protruded from the top of the box. Something was curled up inside the blanket. Janey heard the sound again—a wheezy whine—as the blanket shifted slightly.

"It's an animal!" Janey called out to Zach. "I think it's hurt."

Zach hopped off the milk crate and joined her. "Be careful," he told Janey. He'd heard plenty of stories from his mother about people getting injured trying to

rescue animals. "If it's scared, it may try to bite."

"We're here to help," Janey said in gentle tones as she leaned over the bundle. The creature stirred, a gray snout poking out from the folds of the blanket. "It's a dog," Janey said as its face came further into view. Cloudy brown eyes stared up at them from droopy eyelids. "He looks sick."

"And scared," Zach added. "He's shivering, even though it's a sunny day." He looked around for help, but there was no one else in the alley. They could go inside the gym, but would the people there know how to handle the situation? He straightened, knowing what he had to do. "We're not far from my mom's office. I'll run there and get her. Can you stay here and keep watch?"

Janey's stomach twisted in knots as she got a better view of the animal's skinny frame. "Yes. But Zach, please hurry."

. . . .

An hour later, Janey was pacing the floor of Dr. Goldman's waiting room while Zach flipped through a comic book. "I wonder what's going on in there," she said, glancing at the closed door that led to the exam rooms. "I wish we could help."

"We did help," Zach said. "You heard my mom. If we hadn't found the dog, he could've died. Now we have to let her and Micah do their jobs." Micah was a veterinary assistant who worked part-time at the clinic. He'd just come on duty when Zach had arrived, breathless from running, and told his mother and Micah about the dog behind the dumpster. Micah had helped transport the dog back to the clinic and was now assisting with the exam.

Janey knew the dog was in good hands but couldn't stop worrying. She'd seen the look of alarm on Dr. Goldman's face when she'd first set eyes on the bone-thin dog. "What do you think happened to him?" Janey asked Zach.

Before he could respond, the door opened and Dr. Goldman emerged. Her expression was grim as she told the kids, "She's in pretty bad shape—dehydrated and extremely malnourished."

Zach looked up from his comic book. "She?"

"Yes. Our patient is a female pit bull mix. About two years old, I'd say."

"She's going to be okay, isn't she?" Janey asked.

Dr. Goldman bit her lip. "She's very weak. Her breathing is shallow, and she has a severe infection in both ears. We've started her on fluids and antibiotics. But I have to be honest—it's touch and go."

"You mean . . . she could die?" Zach asked.

"The next twelve hours are critical," his mother told him. "If she makes it through the night, she'll have a fighting chance."

Janey felt queasy upon hearing this news. "That sounds pretty dire." She glanced at Zach, whose glum expression didn't change. She knew he must be worried if he didn't tease her about trying out a new vocabulary word. Janey loved using interesting words. "Dire" described a situation that was serious or urgent. She looked back at Zach's mother. "Can we see her?"

The doctor shook her head. "Why don't you come back in the morning when she's cleaned up and rested."

Micah came out of the exam room. The veterinary assistant was in his early twenties, with close-cropped brown hair and a face dotted with freckles. He held a tube of ointment in his gloved hands.

"Should I put some of this on her toe pads? They're all dry and cracked."

"Yes. Thanks, Micah." Dr. Goldman looked at her watch and then back over at the veterinary assistant. "I'm going to drive Zach and Janey home and grab some dinner, then I'll be back to check on her again. In the meantime, call me on my cell phone if there's any change in her condition."

Janey swirled spaghetti on her fork as she told her parents about the sick dog. She'd only eaten a few bites of her dinner. Every time she pictured the pup's face staring up at her from the cardboard box, her stomach churned with worry. Finally she asked to be excused so she could call Adam and Lolli.

Adam was horrified to hear about the dog's condition. "What's her name?"

"We don't know. She wasn't wearing a collar or tags."

After checking with his mother, Adam told Janey he'd be there in the morning when they went to check on the dog. "Maybe there's something the Pet Rescue Club can do to help her."

"Good idea. I'll ask Lolli to come, too,"

Janey said before hanging up.

"Behind the gym on Bailey Street? But what kind of person would leave a dog in a cardboard box?" Lolli wanted to know when Janey had finished telling her the story. "It's a good thing you and Zach found her when you did."

"I know," Janey agreed. "I just hope we weren't too late."

4

Good News

Zach, Adam, and Lolli were already at the clinic when Janey's mother dropped her off the next morning. The four friends huddled outside the exam room door, waiting anxiously as Zach's mother examined her nameless patient.

"She made it through the night," Lolli said. "That's a good sign, right?"

The door opened and Dr. Goldman stepped out, a stethoscope draped around her neck and a clipboard tucked under one arm. She led the kids into an adjoining room before speaking. "She's looking much better this morning. I think she's going to be okay."

The children cheered at the news. Zach pumped his fist in the air. "Yeah!"

His mother put a finger to her lips. "Let's keep our voices down. Dogs that have been abused tend to startle easily. We want to keep her calm."

"Abused?" Lolli covered her open mouth with one hand.

The doctor nodded. "This dog shows signs of serious neglect as well as abuse. Someone somewhere was very mean to her."

Adam asked the question that was on all their minds. "What can we do to help her?"

"Plenty. For starters, she's going to need a lot of TLC."

"Tender loving care is our specialty," Lolli said, earning smiles of approval from the rest of the gang. "We can play with her, spoil her silly, take her for walks, and help nurse her back to health."

"And when she's all better, we'll find her a new home," Janey added. She let out a sigh filled with longing. "I wish I could keep her, but—"

"Your dad is allergic," Zach finished for her. "We know, we know. And Adam's landlord won't allow pets, and both my parents and Lolli's think we have enough animals already. Besides, if we adopted every animal we rescued, we'd fill a zoo!"

They heard footsteps in the hall, and a moment later, Micah popped his head into the room. "You're here early," Dr. Goldman told him. "Your shift doesn't begin for two hours."

"I know. I wanted to check on the Bailey Street dog. I've been worried about her all night." He raised a hand to his mouth, covering a yawn.

"She's going to be fine." Dr. Goldman consulted the notes on her clipboard. "Her temperature came down overnight, and her lungs sound clear. She even managed to keep a little bit of food down this morning." She looked over at Zach. "Would you bring me a folder from the supply cabinet? We need to start a file on this patient."

Zach often helped his mother with paperwork around the office. He slid through the door and returned moments later with a manila folder and a marker. "What should I write on the label? She doesn't have a name."

"Someone around town must know her," his mother said. "We'll try to find out who she is and what happened to her. In the meantime, let's give her a new name. We can't keep calling her the Bailey Street dog."

"How about Bailey for short?" Lolli suggested.

They all liked the sound of that. Zach wrote the name in neat black letters on the file folder and handed it to his mother. "Now may we see her?"

. . . .

Bailey was curled up on a cushion in the corner of her kennel. Her ratty green blanket had been replaced with a new blue

one. Janey crouched beside the dog and spoke in hushed tones. After a moment, Bailey lifted her head slightly and blinked up at her. Gazing into the dog's round brown eyes, Janey smiled, detecting a spark in them that had been absent the day before. The rest of the dog's appearance had also improved. Her short gray fur—filthy when they'd found her—now looked glossy and clean. And while she still seemed weak, she was no longer shivering in distress.

After a moment, Bailey lowered her head and closed her eyes. Janey stood and backed away from the kennel, careful not to make any sudden movements that could frighten the dog.

Under the watchful eye of Dr. Goldman,

the kids were taking turns visiting Bailey. "It could take a long time before she trusts people again," the vet had cautioned them. "Meeting all four of you at once could be overwhelming."

As Janey was leaving the kennel room, Micah appeared in the doorway. "Um, the cops are here," he told Dr. Goldman.

Janey gasped. Why would the police be at the clinic?

"Actually, just one cop," Micah continued. "A tall guy. He's in the waiting room."

. . . .

"It's my duty to report any signs of animal abuse or abandonment to the police," Dr. Goldman explained to the kids before giving her statement to Chief Mario Pedroche.

The chief wrote a detailed report of Bailey's condition, even sketching the block where the dog was found. "Does that look right?" he asked, showing the map to Zach and Janey.

"Yes," Zach said, pointing. "Between the dumpster and this wall here."

"Will you be able to find out where she lives and what happened to her?" Lolli asked.

The chief scratched his head. "We'll investigate, but sadly, most cases like these are a dead end. Some people who can no longer care for their pets abandon them, instead of doing the right thing and surrendering them to the shelter. We've found animals that were left in the woods or at the shopping center or in empty apartments after the tenants moved out. But now that I have a description, I'll ask around, see if anyone recognizes this dog."

Zach had a thought. "Adam has a dog-walking and pet-sitting business. So he knows practically every dog in town." He turned to Adam and asked, "Does Bailey look familiar to you?"

They all looked over at Adam, who shook his head. "I only know one other pit bull, and he's white, not gray—and way bigger than Bailey."

Janey sighed. "That's too bad."

"Yes, but it was an excellent question," the chief said with a nod in Zach's direction. "You've got good investigative instincts. Are you still thinking about a career as a detective?"

Zach beamed. "Yeah, I think so."

Chief Pedroche signed his report and then separated the pages, handing one to Dr. Goldman. "Here's your copy." He walked to the front door and then paused, turning back to the group. "Like I said, we may never learn who is responsible for Bailey's suffering. But we can make sure she has a brighter future ahead of her."

"That's where we come in," Lolli said, with a gesture that included her three friends. "The Pet Rescue Club is on the case!"

5

Extra Credit

"What's in the box?" Janey asked as Adam made his way down the aisle toward her desk. His backpack was slung over one shoulder and he carried a large rectangular box in both hands.

"Extra credit," came his reply.

For their Career Day assignment, the students in Mrs. Parrett's English class wrote an essay about one of the professions they had learned about. Janey's paper, "Why I Want to Be a Veterinarian," was typed and sitting on the edge of her desk. She'd included photos of Dr. Goldman and some of her patients. Her favorite picture was of Bailey. It had been taken a week after her rescue, when her ears were still badly infected. The vet had fastened a plastic cone around Bailey's neck to prevent her from scratching her ears. It looked like the dog had stuck her head through a lampshade!

Adam set his backpack on his desk and brought the box over to Janey, lifting the lid so she could see the contents.

"Cookies?" she asked, not entirely certain what the misshapen brown lumps in the box were supposed to be.

"Of course they're cookies. Mrs. Parrett said we could earn extra points by doing a

career-related project. So I created an original recipe. I call them Adam's Originals—Version 2.0."

Zach and Lolli entered the classroom and Adam called them over. "Try a cookie. I made enough for the whole class plus a few extras."

"Gee, thanks, but I don't want to spoil my lunch," Janey said.

"I'm game," Zach said, grabbing a cookie and taking a bite.

Lolli did the same. "Me, too."

Adam and Janey watched their expressions change as they chewed. "Well?" Adam asked anxiously. "Should I make more for the bake sale?"

Zach grimaced as he swallowed. "Ugh. Tastes like charcoal and chocolate."

"That's a step up from charcoal and chalk," Adam said with a good-natured chuckle.

"Definitely better than the last batch," Lolli said, then hesitated.

"But . . . ?" Adam prompted her.

"They're kind of dry and crumbly. And a little bit burnt on the bottom." She tilted her head to one side. "I'm sorry, Adam. I'm sure the next batch will be great."

The bell rang, and Mrs. Parrett called the class to attention. "Career Day essays are due today. Please pass your papers to the front of each row."

. . . .

When class ended, Adam carried the box of uneaten cookies over to the trash can. A few students had tried them, but none liked them. At least he'd earned extra credit points for the effort.

He was about to dump the box in the trash when Zach startled him, slapping him on the back. "Hey, don't throw those out. Bring them to gym class instead. We can use them as hockey pucks!" Zach bent over in laughter at his own joke.

Janey rolled her eyes. "Don't listen to him."

"He's right," Adam said with a shrug. "Maybe I shouldn't be a baker."

They exited the classroom and headed toward the cafeteria. As they walked, Lolli asked Zach if he had any news on Bailey.

Zach nodded. "My mom said she's

getting stronger every day. Pretty soon she'll be well enough to move to the shelter. She says that's when our real work with Bailey will begin. We have to help her get used to people and other animals before she can be adopted."

"I can introduce her to Roscoe," Lolli offered. "He's great with other dogs."

They reached the cafeteria and Lolli headed for their usual table. Since she always brought her lunch from home, she saved seats for the others while they stood in line for their food.

Janey grabbed a tray and made her way through the lunch line, selecting mini-dogs, tots, and a piece of carrot cake. The carrot cake looked especially delicious and made her think of the bake sale they were planning. "Maybe we should increase our fundraising goal for the bake sale," she told Adam and Zach as they carried their trays to the table. "And we can use some of the money to help Bailey."

Zach tossed a tot into the air and caught

it in his mouth. "Good idea. We can make posters with his picture on them and put them up in the neighborhood. That'll draw more customers to our sale."

"I can add information about Bailey to my blog," Janey added. "With links to websites about preventing animal cruelty. And I'll e-mail his photo to that newspaper reporter who spoke at Career Day."

Lolli unscrewed the cap of her water bottle and took a sip. "If we want to raise more money, we'll need more stuff to sell."

Janey pushed her tray aside and reached for her notebook. "I'll make a list of people we can ask for help. We each probably have friends or neighbors who know how to bake."

"Put Mr. Mulligan on that list," Adam said, tapping Janey's notebook. "I'll visit his bakery after school and ask if he'll donate some pastries."

"Great idea, Adam," Lolli and Janey said in unison.

"Yeah," Zach added, "and while you're there, why don't you ask him for baking lessons!"

6

Busy Day

"When it rains, it pours," Kitty told Janey and Lolli as they spread a checkered tablecloth over a table they'd positioned in front of the Third Street Animal Shelter. It was the Saturday of the bake sale, and the girls were the first of the club members to arrive. Kitty, their favorite shelter worker, helped the girls arrange the baked goods for the sale.

Janey looked up at the clear blue sky. "The weather man said nothing about precipitation this weekend. "Precipitation was another one of Janey's new favorite words. It was more fun to say than rain.

"If it rains, all of our goodies will turn to mush," Lolli fretted.

"It's not going to rain," Kitty reassured them. "That's just a saying. It means that things tend to happen all at once, like today. We've got the bake sale as well as our usual duties, and Dr. Goldman just called to say she's going to release Bailey to our care at the shelter this morning."

"Great news," Lolli told Adam when he arrived moments later pulling a red wagon filled with bakery boxes. "Bailey's all better!"

Kitty held up both hands. "That's not

quite true. Her physical wounds have healed, but it can take a lot longer to recover from the emotional effects of abuse."

Janey nodded grimly. Since finding Bailey, she'd often imagined how the dog must have felt in that box behind the dumpster—starving, shivering, and all alone. She never wanted her to feel that way again. "We'll show her lots of love. And help her learn to trust people again."

"She's lucky to have the Pet Rescue Club on her side," Kitty said with a smile. "I need to go inside and get her kennel ready. I'll be back soon."

The girls helped Adam unload his wagon. Lolli lifted the lid on one of the pastry boxes and squealed with excitement.

"These cake pops are decorated to look like kittens and puppies! I bet we sell out of these, lickety-split."

"*Awww*, the cupcakes have animal faces, too," Janey said, peeking into another container. "And these croissants look delicious. Wow! Adam, you really came through. These will help us raise a lot of money."

Adam beamed with pride. "Mr. Mulligan donated most of this stuff from his bakery. He loves animals and was happy to help." He lifted the last box from his wagon and set it on the table. It was labeled ADAM'S ORIGINALS—VERSION 3.0. "These aren't as fancy as the stuff from the bakery, but I think they turned out pretty good."

Lolli's eyes widened in surprise as she gazed at the contents of the box—dozens of cookies, golden brown and perfectly round. "I can't wait to try one." She reached into her pocket and pulled out a dollar bill. "How much are they?"

"We put Zach in charge of pricing." Adam looked around. "Where is he?"

"That's his mother's car." Janey pointed

at a blue vehicle that had just pulled to the curb. The passenger door opened and Zach hopped out, carrying his backpack and a box of store-bought doughnuts. He handed them off to Adam and then returned to the car to help his mother with Bailey.

"She's still quite timid," Dr. Goldman told the kids as she lifted the dog from the backseat. "Let's stick to one-on-one visits for today, okay? In a few days we can start introducing her to larger groups."

"We'll take turns staffing the bake sale and sitting with Bailey," Janey said to her friends. "Who wants to go first? Zach, we need your help with pricing."

"I'll go." Lolli tucked her dollar back into her pocket. She held the door to the shelter open for Dr. Goldman, who carried Bailey inside. "Save me one of Adam's cookies," Lolli said over her shoulder. "I'm dying to try them."

"You might be dying after you try them," Zach joked.

. . . .

Their first customer arrived before they'd finished setting up. Miss Evelyn from the church couldn't decide between four different flavors of pastries, so she bought one of each.

Over the next few hours they greeted a steady stream of customers. Some had read about the bake sale online or in the newspaper, while others happened upon it during a Saturday stroll or shopping trip. The florist came out of his shop next door to buy a couple of cupcakes. Adam's neighbors, the Butterfields, bought some of Lolli's organic dog treats for their pets, Digger and Champion. Janey took photos throughout the day, planning to post the best ones on her blog.

At noon, she went inside to relieve Zach, who'd been sitting with Bailey in the Meet-and-Greet room. When she arrived, she had to giggle. Zach was reading aloud to the dog from one of his comic books!

Zach looked up at the sound of her approach. "Lolli sang to her, and Adam played his harmonica. So I read to her. I think she likes comics." The dog's head was resting on

Zach's lap and she looked perfectly at peace.

Janey smiled and said, "I think you're right." When Zach left the room, Bailey began to whine. Janey pet the dog and spoke softly to her until she quieted down. "It's okay, girl. I'm right here. I didn't bring a book to read or an instrument to play, but I can tell you stories. Would you like that?" As if answering her question, Bailey licked her hand.

. . . .

Chief Pedroche, who stopped by the bake sale in the afternoon, purchased a dozen brownies for the crew at the police station and a blueberry muffin for himself. "Isn't that Bailey?" he asked, pointing at one of the posters hanging from the front of the table.

"Yep, she's our poster pooch," Zach told him. "Part of the money we're raising will help pay for her care."

Janey patted the cash box in front of her. "We'd hoped to raise two hundred dollars, but we're not even close."

"Every dollar counts. You kids should be proud of yourselves." The chief talked to them for a while longer and was pleased to learn that Bailey had improved enough to move to the shelter. Then he reached for his wallet again. "I'll take a few of those cake pops, too."

Pretty soon they were down to a handful of items, including the last of Adam's original cookies. "Try one," Adam urged Zach. "On the house."

"No, thanks. I made that mistake twice already."

"They're really good," Lolli insisted. "I had one this morning. Janey did, too. She said they were fab."

Zach remained skeptical. "They don't taste like charcoal and chalk?"

"More like . . . chocolate and cherries," Lolli said.

"They're delicious!" Zach said when he finished the cookie. "What gives?"

Adam pushed his glasses back on his nose. "I asked Mr. Mulligan for some advice. Instead of starting completely from scratch, he said I should take a proven recipe and slowly make adjustments. So I added candied cherries to a traditional chocolate chip cookie recipe. And voilá!"

Kitty helped the kids carry the tables and supplies back inside the shelter. Then the gang gathered in the office to tally the money. Kitty tipped the cash box over on her desk and began sorting the bills and coins. In the middle of the pile was an envelope with the words FOR BAILEY written on the outside. "What's this?"

"Looks like someone made a donation." Lolli tore open the envelope and gasped. "Fifty dollars! I wonder who put that in there?"

None of the kids had noticed anyone slip an envelope into the cash box, but it had been a busy day with too many customers to count. "It could have been anyone," Janey said finally.

Kitty looked up from her counting. "One hundred fifty-eight. With the fifty-dollar donation, the total comes to two hundred eight dollars."

Janey and Lolli hugged, and Adam shouted, "Yippee!"

"I guess we'll never know who made the donation," Kitty said. "Since they didn't include their name."

"It's a mystery, all right." Zach picked the envelope up off the desk and turned it over in his hands. Then, recalling what Chief Pedroche had said about his investigative instincts, he smiled and said, "I think I'll try to solve it."

7

Zach the Detective

"Have you figured out who Bailey's secret benefactor is yet?" Janey asked as she fell into step beside Zach. Three weeks had passed since Bailey moved to the shelter, and the club members had established a routine for her care that included daily walks around the neighborhood. Today was Janey and Zach's turn, so when school let out, they walked the few blocks to the shelter together.

"Bailey's *what?*" Zach asked with a smirk.

"A benefactor is someone who gives money to a person or a cause," Janey explained. "You know, kind of like Bailey's anonymous donor."

Zach rolled his eyes. "Why didn't you just say that in the first place? You don't always have to use weird words." They waited at a crosswalk for the light to change. "And no, I haven't figured it out. But I have a plan. I looked through all the photos you took at the bake sale, and I made a list of everyone in them. Now I just have to narrow down the list of suspects."

"How are you going to do that?"

Zach smiled slyly. "You'll see."

. . . .

"Bailey has a new neighbor," Kitty announced when they arrived at the shelter. They'd kept the kennels closest to Bailey empty for the first few weeks while she gradually got accustomed to being around other dogs. "A Boston terrier named Rocky whose owner passed away. He's an older dog, and very calm, so we thought we'd put him next to Bailey to see how they got along."

"And? How's it going?" Zach asked.

"Terrific." Kitty opened the door to the dog room and led the way down the aisle. "They've been sniffing each other through the bars. No growling or barking." She handed a leash to Zach and opened the door to Bailey's kennel.

As Zach prepared Bailey for their walk, Janey crouched next to the adjacent kennel and smiled at the black-and-white terrier inside. "Hello, Rocky. It's nice to meet you. Maybe next time we'll take you along on a walk."

Outside the shelter, Janey gripped Bailey's leash as she looked up and down the street. "Which way should we go today?" Before Zach could answer, Bailey strained at her leash in the direction of the post office. Janey laughed. "I guess she's made up her mind."

Adam's neighbors, Mr. and Mrs Butterfield, were just exiting the post office. Where Bailey had once been skittish around strangers, she now seemed to enjoy greeting the people they encountered. The Butterfields were no exception. Bailey trotted right up to them and let them pat her head.

"She's grown so much more confident since we saw her last," Mrs. Butterfield said.

"She sure has," Janey agreed.

"Would you both mind signing my yearbook?" Zach asked, reaching into his backpack.

"We'd be honored." Mr. Butterfield stroked his trim gray beard. "But aren't

yearbooks meant to be signed by your school friends and teachers?"

Janey looked smug. "And Zach says I'm the weird one."

"My friends and teachers have already signed it. Now I'm collecting signatures around the neighborhood." Zach handed them the book and a pen and watched as they each wrote their name and a brief message. "Thanks!"

After the couple rounded the corner, Zach reached into his pocket and pulled out an envelope. The words FOR BAILEY were written on the front. He compared the writing on the envelope to the Butterfields' signatures in his yearbook. "No match."

"Aha! So that's your plan to find our

mystery donor." Janey cast an admiring glance in Zach's direction. "Very clever."

As they walked through town, Zach collected four additional signatures, but none matched the writing on the envelope. "Maybe you shouldn't try to find out who gave the money," Janey said when Bailey stopped to sniff the bushes in front of the church.

"But aren't you curious?" Zach asked.

"Yes, but the person must have had their reasons for keeping it secret." She gave Bailey's leash a gentle tug. "Time to head back to the shelter." The dog wouldn't budge. Janey tugged the leash more firmly. "Come, Bailey."

"Let me try." Zach took the leash from

Janey and tried to lead the dog away from the church, but Bailey held her ground and began to bark. "What's wrong, girl? Why won't you move?"

Then Bailey did move, but instead of continuing down Main Street, she pulled Zach around the side of the church. Her barks grew louder. The dog was much stronger than when they'd first found her, and Zach struggled to get her under control. Janey hurried after them. "I wonder what's gotten into her? She rarely barks anymore."

The small parking lot behind the church was empty except for one car. Janey gasped when she saw that the car's trunk was open and a ripped grocery bag lay on the asphalt, its contents spilled all around.

Bailey had stopped barking, and her short ears were pointing straight up. Zach and Janey finally heard what had attracted the dog's attention—a woman's soft cries. They ran to the other side of the car and found Miss Evelyn on the ground, clutching her ankle. "I slipped and fell," the woman said between sobs. "My ankle . . . I think it's sprained."

8

Good Neighbor

Lolli straightened her shirt collar and smoothed her curly black hair. Being invited to a ceremony at Town Hall was a big deal, and she wanted to look her best. The other members of the Pet Rescue Club were seated beside her in the front row. Their families and other members of the community were also in the audience.

Chief Pedroche stepped to the podium and adjusted the microphone. "Thank you all for coming to this unusual event. As many of you know, the police department awards a Neighborly Medal to folks who do good deeds around town." He held up a gold medal suspended from a blue ribbon. Flashes of light popped around the room as people snapped pictures.

"Today it is my privilege to bestow this award on a true hero who came to the rescue of Miss Evelyn Wakefield, the music director of our church. Miss Wakefield fell and sprained her ankle while unloading groceries for the church potluck. She was lying on the ground for more than an hour because no one heard her cries for help." The chief's voice broke as he choked back tears. "No one, that is, but Bailey—the first animal to ever win the Neighborly Medal."

He turned and gestured toward the back of the room. At his signal, Kitty came forward, leading Bailey on her leash. When they reached the podium, Bailey sat at attention. The crowd cheered as the chief draped the medal around the dog's neck.

The chief continued, "I would also like to acknowledge the members of the Pet Rescue Club, who helped nurse Bailey back to health after she was abandoned in an alley. Kids, come on up here."

Zach, Adam, Lolli, and Janey stood and made their way to the podium, lining up next to Bailey and Kitty. The chief went down the row and shook each of their hands.

"Excuse me, Chief Pedroche?" Cara

Panero, the newspaper reporter who'd spoken at Career Day, stood in the aisle, a large camera hanging from a strap around her neck. "May I get a group photo for the paper?"

. . . .

"I can't wait to see our picture in the newspaper," Lolli said later that day. She and Adam had returned to the shelter with Kitty. Even though Bailey had already had a big day, they wanted to stick to her schedule of daily walks around the neighborhood.

Adam nodded. "And maybe the story about Bailey being a hero will help her find a new home."

The phone on Kitty's desk rang. Knowing that Kitty was in the back giving a kitten a flea bath, Lolli picked up the receiver. "Third Street Animal Shelter, this is Lolli speaking."

A woman's voice came over the line. "Hello, I was wondering . . . well, I have a question about ducks."

Lolli recognized the caller's voice. "Miss Evelyn? How are you feeling? Is your ankle getting better?"

"Not yet, I'm afraid. I can't get around very well on my crutches, so I've been laid up at home. It's sweet of you to ask."

"We've all been concerned about you." Lolli told her about Bailey's award ceremony then asked, "Did you say you have a question about ducks?"

"Indeed." Since her injury, Miss Evelyn had been unable to walk down to the stream behind her property to feed the ducks. She told Lolli she sat by her window each morning, hoping to catch a glimpse of them. "The mama duck has seven fuzzy little ducklings, and I love to watch them follow her around."

Lolli sighed happily. "Ducklings are the cutest!"

"Well this afternoon, I heard quacking coming from my backyard. I looked out the window and there's mama duck marching in circles and flapping her wings, but her ducklings are nowhere in sight. Is that normal?"

"I don't think so," Lolli said. "They stick pretty close to their mother. They could be in trouble. Let me see if I can get Kitty or one of the other shelter workers to come to the phone." She put her hand over the receiver and spoke to Adam. When she'd told him about Miss Evelyn's concerns, Adam went to find Kitty.

"*Quackity quack*," Miss Evelyn was saying when Lolli resumed the conversation. "It's like she's trying to tell me something. But heaven knows what."

Lolli frowned, picturing the distressed duck. "She's walking around in circles?"

"Well, one big circle. Around my pool."

"There's a pool in your backyard?"

Lolli asked. "Is it a big one, or a little kiddie pool?"

Miss Evelyn laughed. "Not a kiddie pool, no. I don't have children. It's a full-size pool."

Kitty emerged from the back room, drying her hands on a towel. Lolli held one finger in the air and continued her line of questioning. "Is it covered?"

"No. I was planning to swim this weekend, but then I sprained my ankle, so—"

Lolli interrupted her. "I've heard of ducks getting into people's swimming pools. If the ducklings are little they might not be able to get out on their own."

"Oh my!" Miss Evelyn sounded worried. "I can't see into the pool from my window. And I really shouldn't try to walk on this ankle."

"No, no, stay where you are."

Lolli passed the phone to Kitty, who asked a few questions of her own before saying, "What's your address? We'll be right over."

Miss Evelyn watched from her window as Kitty, Adam, and Lolli made their way across the backyard to her swimming pool. Lolli's hunch had been right: Seven yellow ducklings were indeed stuck in the pool. They'd most likely followed their mother in for a swim, but unlike her they couldn't fly and were too small to climb out.

Adam dipped his hands into the pool and attempted to scoop up a duckling, but it quickly swam out of reach. The bird peeped in alarm, and the rest joined in the chorus. "The poor things are afraid of me.

How will we catch them?"

"What if we drain the pool?" Lolli suggested.

"The best thing we can do is build a ramp so they can climb out on their own." Kitty looked around the backyard, smiling when she saw a beach towel draped over a lawn chair. "These will do." A few minutes later, she'd pulled the lawn chair over to the edge of the pool. She tipped it over and positioned it so that it was half in and half out of the water. Then she moistened the towel and laid it across the chair. "The wet towel will provide traction for slippery feet," she said in response to Lolli's and Adam's curious looks.

Meanwhile, the mother duck's quacks had intensified. "She's agitated," Kitty said.

"She doesn't know that we're here to help her babies rather than hurt them. Let's go inside and watch from the window with Miss Evelyn."

Once the coast was clear, the ducklings slowly made their way up the makeshift ramp. From her chair by the window, Miss Evelyn counted as, one by one, the ducklings popped into view. She thanked Kitty and the kids for their help, then they all watched as the mother duck waddled out of the yard, her feathered flock following close behind.

9

Wonder Dog

"Bailey's a star!" Janey said as she spread the Sunday paper on her family's kitchen counter. Her parents stood on either side of her, smiles wide as they stared down at the front page. Beneath a headline reading "A Dog-gone Hero" was a photo of Bailey, the gleaming gold medal around her neck. A second picture showed the dog surrounded by Chief Pedroche and the members of the Pet Rescue Club.

"So are you." Her mother wrapped an arm around Janey's shoulders. "And your friends."

"We're proud of you, sweetheart," her father said.

Janey read the newspaper article as she ate a celebratory breakfast of banana pancakes and bacon. The reporter did a great job describing Bailey's background and personality, Janey thought as she brought a forkful of food to her mouth. She wouldn't be surprised if the dog was adopted right away.

A few minutes later a horn honked in the driveway, and Janey hurried to the window. Lolli waved to her from the backseat of her parents' station wagon. Mr. and Mrs. Simpson were attending an organic food festival and had offered to drop off the girls for their shift at the shelter on the way. Eager to see Bailey, Janey quickly kissed her parents and dashed out the door.

On the drive to the shelter, Lolli told Janey about the duck-saving adventure of the day before.

"Those poor ducklings must have been hungry and tired," Janey said. She shivered to think of what might have happened if Miss Evelyn hadn't realized the ducklings were missing until it was too late. "I hope they don't decide to go back for another swim."

"We covered up the pool before we left," Lolli told her. "And Kitty called Ms. Winkins from the hardware store. She has a critter rescue ramp in stock, and she's going to install it for Miss Evelyn."

"A critter rescue ramp? I never knew

there was such a thing," Janey said.

Lolli nodded. "I guess all sorts of animals get trapped in swimming pools. Kitty gave Miss Evelyn some tips on how to prevent wildlife from getting in her pool in the first place."

"Kitty sure knows her stuff," Janey said admiringly. "She should speak at our school's next Career Day. Being a shelter worker is an awesome job."

When they entered the Third Street Animal Shelter, they found Kitty at the front desk. "The phone's been ringing off the hook," she told them, tucking a stray blond hair back into her ponytail. "Because of that newspaper story, lots of people are interested in adopting Bailey."

"That's great!" Janey said.

A bell tinkled and she turned to see a

family of four come through the shelter's front door. A boy of about five or six shouted, "I want Bailey!"

"Bailey, Bailey," echoed his sister, a toddler whose matching hair was done up in pigtails.

Their mother addressed Kitty, who had come out from behind the desk to greet them. "We called earlier. About Bailey, obviously," she added with a weary smile.

Her husband pointed toward the front window. "My van's right out front. So we can take the dog home today."

"First you can meet her, and we'll see how that goes." Kitty turned to Lolli. "Please bring them to the Meet-and-Greet room, and I'll go get Bailey."

The phone rang and Janey said, "I'll

get it." She hurried toward the desk and reached for the phone. "I was right. Bailey is a star!"

. . . .

"Bailey!" the red-headed girl shouted when Kitty brought the dog into the room. She gave Bailey an enthusiastic embrace and squealed when the dog licked her face. Then her brother rushed forward and both siblings pet Bailey's back and rubbed her belly. The dog was enjoying the attention until one of the children accidentally pet a little too close to Bailey's ear. Bailey gave a sharp warning bark, and the little girl burst into tears.

Her father pulled the girl away, sweeping her into his arms to comfort her.

"Bailey had a bad ear infection, she's especially sensitive right now," Kitty explained.

The mother understood, but her children were already running up to other dogs. "It looks like we're going to look at a few more pups today," she told Kitty as she hurried off.

Over the next two hours, several additional people came to visit Bailey, but none was the right fit. A college-aged girl came close to filling out the adoption application after sitting with the pit bull for a long time. Eventually, she decided her course work kept her too busy to properly care for a dog recovering from abuse.

As they took Bailey out for her afternoon walk, Janey worried that the dog would never find a loving home.

"I have a feeling the right person will come along soon," Lolli reassured her.

On every block, they encountered people who knew Bailey. A couple of teenagers recognized her from the newspaper and called her "Bailey, the

Wonder Dog." Shop owners on Bailey's regular walking route would drop what they were doing when she passed. The dog seemed to have her favorite stops, including the bakery, where Mr. Mulligan would sometimes slip her a treat, and the police station, where the officers on duty would come out to say hello.

"Hey, isn't that Adam? Lolli pointed down the street at a boy with glasses who was standing under the awning of Mulligan's Bakery.

"Yes, that's him," Janey said as they got closer. Bailey trotted forward to greet their friend, who blushed when they asked what he was doing at the bakery.

"I took a cake decorating class." He

folded his hands together. "Please don't tell Zach. He'll tease me like crazy."

Lolli mimed locking her lips and throwing away the key. "It'll be our secret."

"Are you off to walk some dogs?" Janey asked him.

Adam shook his head. "I don't have any

clients today, so I thought I'd head over to the shelter. I figured they'd need extra help because of the newspaper article."

"That's for sure," Janey said. "Why don't you walk with us?"

. . . .

Zach was spending that Sunday helping his mother at the clinic. He cut the front-page story about Bailey from the newspaper and pinned it to the bulletin board in the waiting room. Then he set to work straightening the paperwork that had accumulated on her desk. She'd been so busy she'd fallen behind in her filing, so she'd offered Zach a boost to his allowance if he helped.

He was sorting the papers into separate piles for bills, correspondence, and patient test results, when he came across a copy of the police report regarding Bailey. He remembered Chief Pedroche filling out the form on the day they'd found the dog in the alley.

Zach winced, remembering how scrawny and scared Bailey had been that first day. She'd come a long way since then. Something nagged at the back of his brain as he perused the police report. Then he stood suddenly and went to find his mother.

Dr. Goldman was finishing up her exam of a tabby cat when Zach poked his head through the open door. "I'm taking a break," he told her. "May I go visit the police station?"

10

Mystery Solved

Chief Pedroche smiled when Zach pushed through the glass doors of the police station, skateboard in one hand. "Good to see you, sport. Are you still thinking of becoming a detective?"

"Yes, and I've solved my first case." Zach set down his skateboard and shook the chief's hand. "I know who Bailey's benefactor is."

The chief's smile faded. "What do you mean?"

"A benefactor is someone who gives money to a person or a cause. According to Janey, anyway."

"Yes, I know. But—"

Zach pulled a wrinkled envelope from his back pocket and set it on the counter. Though the ink had faded, the words FOR BAILEY were still visible on the front. He then withdrew a folded piece of paper from another pocket. "This is a copy of your report about Bailey," he said, unfolding it and placing it next to the envelope. On the top line of the police report, the chief had written the dog's name in capital letters. The handwriting on the two pieces of paper was identical. "You made the mystery donation, didn't you?"

The chief nodded slowly. "Good detective work," he said at last. "That dog really got to me, and I wanted to help her.

I did it anonymously because I didn't want to feel pressured to adopt her." He pointed up at a large framed photo hanging on the wall. It was a picture of a German shepherd. "Ever since Maggie died, people keep asking me when I'm going to get another dog. But I just can't do it. It hurts too much to lose them."

"I understand." Zach folded the papers and slid them back inside his pocket. "You must have loved her very much." He picked up his skateboard and turned to leave. "Thanks for the donation. It really helped."

Zach was nearing the double glass doors when he saw his friends approaching the station with Bailey. Actually, it appeared that the dog was leading the way. He opened the

door and Bailey burst through, followed by Janey, Lolli, and Adam.

"Well, the gang's all here," the chief said.

"It was Bailey's idea," Lolli said. "We tried taking a different route today, but she kept pulling us in this direction. The station is one of her favorite places to visit."

Lolli let go of Bailey's leash and the dog bounded over to the chief, jumping up on her hind legs and nearly knocking him over with her front paws.

"Whoa, girl." Chief Pedroche crouched down and put his arms around Bailey, who waggled her body with obvious delight.

"She really likes you," Janey told the chief. "Are you sure you don't want to—"

"Shhh." Zach pressed a finger to his

lips and whispered, "It's a sore subject." He looked at the chief. "Sorry. She can be so pushy."

"Pushy?" Janey put one hand on her hip. "What are you doing here anyway, Zach? I didn't expect to see you at the police station."

Zach cast a sidelong glance at the chief. "I, um . . ."

"He's been talking about being a detective ever since Career Day," Adam reminded Janey. "He probably came to get some advice."

A handful of police officers had come out of their cubicles to pet and fawn over the dog. A female cop whose name badge read HENSLEY bent down and kissed the top of Bailey's head. "It's too bad we can't have another station dog. But no one could ever replace Maggie. Right, Chief?"

"Right." The chief looked around the room. All eyes were on him, but none shined brighter than Bailey's. The dog was staring up at him in utter adoration. "But maybe it is time to let another animal into my heart."

"Really?" Adam said. "Does that mean you'll adopt Bailey?"

The chief nodded and his eyes misted with tears. "If it's okay with the Pet Rescue Club."

The kids shouted their approval and the station crew broke into applause.

Zach pumped a fist in the air. "She'll be a real police pooch!"

"Well, an honorary one," the chief said. "She'll live with me when she's not at the station."

"And since the shelter is nearby, we'll be able to see her often," Lolli added.

Janey felt a lump rise in her throat as she thought of how close Bailey had come to dying—and how healthy and happy she looked now. They hadn't discovered who was responsible for her suffering or how she wound up in a box behind the gym. She recalled the chief saying that they'd probably never learn about the dog's past, but they could try to ensure she had a brighter future. Thanks to Chief Pedroche and the Pet Rescue Club, Bailey's future was looking bright indeed!

Choose Your Career!

If you are interested in working with animals, there are many different careers you can choose. Look below for a list of possibilities, and take your pick!

Animal Care Technician

Care for animals, including cleaning their kennels, and making sure the animals stay happy and healthy.

Animal Trainer

Help animals (and their humans) learn important things like house or litter box training, walking safely on a leash, using a scratching post, and simple commands like sit, stay, and come!

Humane Educator

Help create communities where pets are safe, valued, and get the loving care they deserve, by sharing information about compassionate care and treatment.

Humane Law Enforcement

Help ensure that pet shops, kennels, stables, and other locations animals are kept follow regulations and deliver proper care.

Lobbyist

Work with government officials and encourage them to pass laws benefitting the welfare of animals.

Office and Support Staff

Assist the people who are working to help animals by sending thank you notes to donors, holding fundraisers, answering phones and email, and helping out around the office.

Pet Adoption Counselor

Match potential owners with shelter pets; and review adoption applications, file paperwork, educate owners, train volunteers, and assist with other shelter duties.

Publications

Help create books, magazines, pamphlets, websites, and social media that encourage respect for and inform people about the well-being of animals.

Service Dog Trainer

Teach dogs to become guide dogs, hearing dogs, or therapy dogs to assist people with disabilities.

Veterinarian

Give medical care and treatment to animals to help them stay healthy.

Veterinary Technician

Help a veterinarian care for his or her patients.

These are just some of the careers that benefit or work with animals. In the meantime, if you're interested in helping animals, visit **www.ASPCA.org** for more information.

Meet the Real Bailey

Bailey, the kindhearted pup, was inspired by a real-life animal rescue story! Zaza, pictured on the left, was rescued by officers from Brooklyn's 63rd Precinct. She was bone-thin when police discovered her living in filthy conditions with another underweight, female pit bull mix. Thankfully, Zaza was taken to the ASPCA Animal Hospital where she was treated for an infection in both ears that caused severe swelling. After months of treatment and care, she was finally ready for a loving home. But first, she had a big day with the NYPD, and joined Police Commissioner William Bratton on the job for "Take Your Dog to Work Day." Following her adventure, Zaza was officially adopted and given a second chance at a loving home.

Look for these other books in the
PET RESCUE CLUB
series!

 1 A New Home for Truman   **2** No Time for Hallie

 3 The Lonely Pony   **4** Too Big to Run   **5** A Puppy Called Disaster

 6 Champion's New Shoes   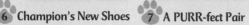 **7** A PURR-fect Pair   **8** Bailey, the Wonder Dog